To Andy

Nina x

WHAT THE CLUCK!

The life and times of a rescue hen

T M Hartup

DEDICATION

This book is dedicated to Babs, Hettie, Chucky, Ginger and Lagatha, our first rescue hens. They introduced us to the world of backyard chicken keeping and the joys of attending to the needs and whims of chooks. Thank you girls.

CHAPTER 1

IN THE BEGINNING

The darkness is lifted and suddenly there is no top lid. The top lid has always been different shades of brown and grey in long stripey planks, sloping downwards towards the edges of the world. The sides were also different shades of brown in long stripey planks. It was sometimes difficult to see the brown top lid with so many of us squeezed in together. With flapping wings and feathers flying it was mostly easier to just sit down on a perch and watch the kerfuffle around me, listening to the squawking.

My first memory was of facing the ground with what I now know was a hooman, holding me by my feet. I was snuggled under a warm heated light with all my brothers and sisters and then suddenly, up I went and off out into the cold, upside down world. I was thrown into my new brown world and joined by lots and lots of sisters. I'm not sure where all my brothers went.

It was very bright in the new brown world. Long strips of white, glaring, shiner lights dominated the brown top lid. For a little while every day the shiners stopped and everything went dark. That made me feel very sleepy.

It was very squashed in the new brown world. With so many of my sisters around, it was often really difficult to find a spot to snuggle down to sleep. I often managed to find a corner on a perch but I was soon pushed up against the edge of the brown world by all my sisters who were shifting along the overcrowded perch. It was sometimes nice to snuggle into a few of my sisters though. If I could manoeuvre myself just inside a fluffy wing or two it felt good.

When the shiner lights burst into life again after a few hours, it was scary. Everyone shouted, screamed and squawked as loud as they could. There was a mad rush to long, reflective, silver troughs where a kind of mashed food came trickling in a steady flow. I had to get there quick to get some crumbs. There were some 'not very nice' sisters who would peck my head to make me get out of the way. I did squeal a bit but they didn't stop so I just ran away as quickly as I could flapping my wings to shove others out of the way.

I did have to tell some of my other sisters off when they got in my way so I pecked their heads as well. I don't know why they squealed, I didn't peck them hard but they did run out of my way.

There were some nice cosy boxes filled with soft, snug, straw bedding with a strange open hole along the back of the brown world. It was lovely sitting in there away from the foul bullies.

On the floor of the brown world was a bit of dark brown dusty dirt that was fun to scratch around in. It was hard finding room for a good scrabble on the ground though, especially with all the poop being squirted around everywhere.

After a few dark, shiner lights off, times the hoomans came in and made us all squeeze up into one side of the brown world while they sprayed smelly water all over the floor. I didn't like that, being pushed into my sisters really tightly. There was lots of pecking and squabbling and some of my sisters ended up with red water oozing out of their skin. That was interesting. Red water looked good. We all had to investigate. When we did investigate, nice tasty bits fell off the skin that we all scrambled to eat. The sisters with red water would usually squawk a bit and sometimes they went to sleep on the floor. The hoomans would then come in and take them away to another world somewhere.

I woke up one morning with terrible tummy ache. I grumbled a bit and wandered about looking for somewhere to snuggle down. I found an empty cosy box so snuggled down in there. Mmmm, it was warm and snug and made me want to purr. My tummy kept hurting a bit and I felt like I had the most enormous poop wanting to come out. I had to push and push and strain to get that hard poop out. And then, What The Cluck! A huge, enormous lump fell out of my bottom. It rolled to the back of the box and then disappeared off down the hole. Wow, what a feeling. Well, I just had to announce that to the world. I had a good clucking sing song about that poop.

From then on, I had regular big poops and I think a lot of my sisters had big poops as well. There was definitely a lot of grumbling and a lot of clucking singing going on in that brown world. It was quite tiring really in that mostly bright, shiny, loud and noisy, world.

One day I woke up on the perch and saw a few of my sisters eyeing me up in a really strange way. They were staring at one of my feathers that was hanging out at a strange angle. One of my sisters pulled at it and, Ouch! What The Cluck! It popped out. I think because I screeched more of my sisters looked at me. Then more started staring at me in an odd way. Their eyes changed to piercing, intently focused pinpoints as they glared at some of my other feathers that were sticking out messily all over my body. They flocked in towards me and all crowded around as they started to pull on some of my other feathers. One came out and one of my beastly sisters gobbled it down. That was painful. It was time to get out of there. I jumped down off the perch but a few of my sisters followed and they then started chasing me. I had to duck and dive all over the place to get away. I found a spot in an empty box where I stayed really still and managed to not be noticed for a good while.

A little later, I looked out from my box and noticed quite a commotion going on everywhere. Lots of my sisters had messy feather styles and they were being chased everywhere. There were feathers and fluff flying all over the place and my sisters were running amok, gobbling them up as they floated in the air. Some of them looked a bit naked with pink, knobbly skin showing through everywhere. A feather floated up near me, I just managed to catch it and gulped it down. It was quite yummy.

I felt ever so tired and my tummy didn't hurt so much but every day more and more feathers were coming out. The hoomans came in more often each day and they kept picking us up and checking us all over. It was all very strange.

Then one morning the shiner lights came on quite early. Lots of hoomans came into our brown world and they started picking my sisters up and putting them in strange red and black plastic boxes with lids. I complained and squawked a bit because it was quite scary. Some of my sisters also complained a bit. I had to squawk a bit louder to make sure that I could be heard complaining. My sisters squawked louder to make themselves heard. It was quite a deafening and rowdy experience. A hooman came near to me and tried to catch me. I got out of there pretty quickly and had to squawk even louder to make it clear I was not happy. I flew up to one of the boxes and hid in there to watch the pandemonium. More and more of my sisters were caught by the hoomans and there were less and less of us left in the brown world. A hooman came towards my box. I pushed myself back as far as I could but the hooman grabbed me and pulled me out. She put me under her arm and although I squirmed and wriggled, I couldn't flap my wings to get away. The hooman opened up the lid of a red plastic box and put me in, closing the lid down on top of me. There were about 9 of my sisters already in there but they were just sat down looking out of the sides of the box. I snuggled into a couple of my sisters and settled down with them. I put my head under my wing. I could not see anything then, which meant that no one could see me.

I heard some hoomans talking together outside of my box. They were squawking about having "homes for these girls" but not being able to "take anymore". Some of the hoomans had wet faces and were talking to my sisters who hadn't yet been caught saying "sorry" or something like that. I looked out at my lucky sisters who had not been caught. They were able to stay in our safe, brown world whilst I was stuck in this small plastic box probably never to flap my wings again or be able to sit on a nice, comfortable perch.

Suddenly the box was lifted and we rose up in the air. We were carried through a strange gap in the brown world into …. What The Cluck! The brown top lid of the world was gone! There was just an immense, vast, blue ceiling over the top of us stretching as far as we could see. There were hoomans everywhere. It was noisy with screeching and clucking squawks and grumbling moaning coming from hundreds of boxes (I speculated that there were hundreds of boxes. Not being able to count, it was a guesstimate). Nearby, there were some huge white, metal, rectangular containers on big, black round things and the boxes carrying me and my sisters was put into one of the white containers. One of the hoomans shouted to other hoomans that "this van is loaded". Being quite astute, I deducted that he was referring to the large white metal container as a van.

I noticed a different, dark green, van with bars on the sides move up, backwards, to our former, brown, world-home. I heard my sisters inside the former, brown, world-home start screaming. Why were they screaming? They were the lucky ones. Then I spotted one of my sisters being caught by her leg as she tried to run outside of the former, brown, world-home. She was picked up... by her leg, upside down and thrown, unceremoniously, into a green, plastic container. She wasn't held under a hooman's arm and put gently into a plastic red or black box. I don't think those girls were going to the same place that we were going. I'm not sure where they were going. And then suddenly I heard a loud bang as something rolled over the back of our container and the world went dark.

What a strange feeling. I tried to stay snuggled into my sisters but the world kept moving up and down and from side to side. It was hard to stay upright and trying to use my wings to steady myself was no help. I was so thirsty but there was nowhere to get a drink. After a while, world suddenly stopped moving. There was another loud noise and then the world was light again. The red plastic box with me and my sisters inside was lifted up in the air again and it was carried somewhere and put down on the floor. Another plastic box, a black one, with some more of my sisters was put over the top of us. Not a good idea when there were holes in the bottom of the boxes - my sisters were scared and their poop was runny.

Wiping the poop off my face and beak, I peered out. More hoomans were coming towards us. The black box over us was taken away and then our red box was lifted up into the air again. We were taken to another metal container but this one was smaller than the big, white van and there were wide transparent windows all around the sides. This time our red box was put on top of my sisters' black box. Payback time! Letting that poop out was a relief. One of my sisters in the box underneath squealed as excrement dripped down through the gaps.

The world started moving again. This time I could see out of the holes in the box through the big open windows of the small van, but I couldn't focus on anything. The world was blurry and fuzzy and I was struggling to stay upright. I looked at my sisters. I think they were feeling the same as there was lots of grumbling going on.

It wasn't very long before the world stopped moving again and our red box was lifted up the air again. We were carried into a strange looking big area with bars on all sides and lots of my sisters were out of their boxes all huddled together in a corner. Our red box was placed on the ground and the lid opened. I popped my head up and saw a chance to escape so I jumped out of the box and ran over to my sisters. Wow, it was amazing to be able to stretch and flap my wings. A good shake, with more feathers dropping out, and then I managed to move into the middle of the huddle and I tried to quietly disappear so that the pesky hoomans wouldn't notice me.

The hoomans soon stopped coming into our cage so I ventured out from the middle of the huddle. I spotted a hanging container with what looked like water slopping about inside so I made a beeline for it. It was a bit of a scramble pushing my sisters out of the way so I could have a drink but I managed with a bit of pecking and ducking and diving. I found some mashed food as well. Woo hoo! Maybe it wouldn't be too bad here. Food, water, some of my sisters for company and I had room to flap my wings. I could see through the bars overhead and the big blue ceiling had changed, there were white fluffy balls moving across it. Very strange.

We all settled and calmed down for a while. The floor was better here than our former, brown, world-home. With a bit of scratching, I found some wriggling, pink meaty worms. And then, wouldn't you know it, along came those pesky hoomans again. They came into our cage and picked up some of my sisters. No matter how much they screamed or tried to flap their wings they couldn't escape and they were taken away and this time, put into strange, small brown boxes. Another hooman came into our cage and picked me up. I tried to get away but it was no use. The hooman was holding my wings tightly against my body and no amount of struggling or squawking could get me free. The hooman put me into one of the boxes and the top was closed down. Suddenly it was dark again. After a few minutes the top was opened up again and one of my sisters joined me. There were all sorts of strange comings and goings outside of our box. I could hear some of my other sisters around and hoomans squawking at each other. "That's your four then. Are you sure you can't take any more. Chicken maths means you should have five". I closed an eye and snuggled down in a corner with my sister. It wasn't long before the world began to move again. What The Cluck… again!

This was a strange new world. Boxes and hoomans and moving worlds and scary cages and fluffy balls in the ceiling and not knowing where to find food and water. I didn't like that world. I wished I was back home in my former, safe, brown world-home.

CHAPTER 2

NEW BEGINNINGS

The world eventually stopped moving and the top of our small, brown box was opened. A pesky hooman lifted me and my sister out and put us into another new world. There was a grey ceiling this time and the cage walls were strange indeed with bars going up, down and across that we could look through. The pesky hoomans went away and I took a look around and saw a few more of my sisters present. It was suddenly very quiet until we heard a loud screech above us. I looked up and saw a strange creature that I'd never seen before floating through the air with big black wings. It made a loud caw-caw noise and flew down to look at us through the see-through cover overhead. Thankfully, it didn't seem to be able to get down to us. I needed to get away from that creature so I

18

followed my sisters, who must have thought the same, and we all ran under a funny shaped, square box thing.

As we ran, I noticed some food in a hanging pot. Well, I remembered where it was and as soon as that big, black caw-caw thing had gone I was straight back there. My sisters came with me and we all crowded around the hanging pot and had a good peck at the lovely food. As the food was devoured and less was left in the pot a couple of my sisters got a bit bossy and pecked my head to get me out of the way. Well, I had to peck a couple of the other girls to get them out of my way. Such is life!

I had my fill, (and wasn't allowed to eat anymore) so I took another look around me. Looking down, I noticed some soft, green floor that was moving. I gave it a scratch and .... What The Cluck! Another long, plump, wriggly worm popped it's head out from the floor. I gobbled that up. Yummy. I scratched again and a tiny, black beetle popped out. Yum. It was well worth a scratch here, so I did it a bit more and, would you believe it, another juicy worm wriggled out. I picked it up in my beak but one of my sisters spotted it and she tried to yank it away from me. I ran off but she chased me and managed to hook the end of my worm in her beak. What a cheek, trying to steal my worm. We had a bit of a tugging war. Wow, …. plump worms stretch out into really, really, long thin worms. I tumbled back a bit as my worm broke and my sister ran off with her winnings. I did manage to get into a corner with my remains though, and gobbled it down before anyone else noticed.

I decided to explore this new world. I found a few hanging food pots, a couple of troughs filled with bubbly water, some pots filled with shells and grit and a lovely, big, open box filled with perfect, bathing dirt. I had to do a few emergency runs under the strange, square shaped box thing whenever we all spotted danger. There were various flying creatures overhead, some of whom became a little too interested in us and sat on the see-through cover overhead. We soon worked out that they couldn't get down to us so we saw them off with a clucking warning.

The grey high ceiling-sky started slowly to change colour and it was getting darker. There didn't seem to be any bright, shiner lights over us so it just became darker and darker. Some of my sisters started to settle on one of the perches that stretch from one side of the cage to the other so thought I'd join them. I was about to snuggle in when those pesky hoomans moved one of the walls and came into our cage. Well, … we flew off that perch pretty quickly and ran under the strange square shaped box where it was a bit safer. We weren't safe though. One of the hoomans picked us out one by one. I squeezed as far into a corner as I could but that pesky hooman reached me and lifted me out, holding my wings down so I couldn't fly away and escape.

The hooman placed me on a brown plank that sloped upwards. "Come on chook, he squawked. This is your new home and you have a lovely, snuggly coop to sleep in." My sisters in front of me were disappearing into a black hole in the 'coop' and the pesky hooman was pushing my bottom, forcing me to follow. Did they really expect me to voluntarily just walk into that dark unknown world and disappear? I certainly clucking grumbled enough so the pesky hooman knew I was not happy.

As I neared the top of the ramp, I could see that my other sisters had not disappeared – in fact they were inside the coop on perches and it actually looked quite snug. I did go in voluntarily and I found a cosy, comfortable place in between a couple of my sisters. A bit of shifting about and manoeuvring into place and we all fit perfectly together in a huddle. The pesky hooman outside was too big to come in so we were safe. The hooman put a wall over the hole where we had come in and suddenly it was dark. I was suddenly very tired and I felt extremely sleepy. I heard the pesky hooman squawking something about "getting names tomorrow". A few of us mumbled an answer, I can't recall but it was something along the lines of "I couldn't give a cluck", as we all dozed off. Phew – what a day!

CHAPTER 3

THE DAWN OF A NEW DAY

I woke, pooped, snuggled back into my sisters, dozed, woke again, pooped, swapped places with one of my sisters, dozed back off, woke up (just the one eye this time), pooped and dozed off again. Shiny light started creeping into our coop. Suddenly the small wall that was put across the opening was moved and glaring light burst in. I had a bit of a leg stretch and my sisters shifted around on the perch, all of us greeting each other with a friendly peck and a quick preen. One of my sisters walked over to the opening. She looked out, she obviously assessed it as safe and went down the ramp. Another of my sisters followed so we all lined up to follow. What world would we be in today?

I walked steadily down the ramp, then I remembered, and noticed, the hanging food pot. Food! I flew off that ramp and was down pecking breakfast before my claws hit the ground. There wasn't much food in the pot though so it was a bit of a struggle to sneak anything from under the beaks of some of my sisters. I noticed a couple of pesky hoomans come out of a big, brick-brown block and come towards us. They were making a weird bop-bop-bop noise and shaking a large bowl. I started to run towards the safe area under the coop but I spotted some food in that hooman's bowl. Food! I decided to bravely stay where I was and I watched as that bowl grew bigger and bigger as it came towards us. I didn't care when those pesky hoomans moved the wall and came into our cage. I stayed focused on that bowl being shaken, filled with wonderful food. One of the pesky hoomans opened the top of the hanging pot and filled it with the delicious food. I was straight in there pecking the scrumptious mashed food. Yummy.

Two hoomans were in our cage. One of them picked up one of my sisters whilst she was trying to eat her breakfast. How rude! She was not happy and she let them know with a clucking squawk. Whilst one of the hoomans held onto her under their arm to stop her from escaping their clutches, the other one put a ring on her leg. They squawked something about her new name being Babs and then she did manage to escape their clutches (or they may have put her down on the ground, I'm not sure).

I thought I'd better get out of there and turned to run to our safe area. Too late. I was lifted up into the air and placed tightly under one of the pesky hoomans arms. I squawked the loudest clucking 'get off me' that I could muster but to no avail. I watched as the other hooman put an orange ring around my leg and screamed in pain. Well, actually, it didn't hurt. I didn't feel it, but it could have hurt so I screamed just in case. The pesky hooman squawked "there you go Ginger, all done" and then I managed to escape their clutches (or they may have put me on the ground I'm not sure).

Soon it seemed that we all had 'names' and different colour leg rings.

The hoomans didn't want to leave our cage for a while. They sat down on four-legged perches that they called 'chairs', holding small troughs of hot liquid that they called 'a cuppa' and they weirdly squawked to us about our 'new home'. They squawked about 'our coop' and about the opening wall being a 'door that we were never to go through'. They clucked about 'other chooks' and 'eggs' and 'being nice to each other'. They kept squawking our 'names' at us and repeatedly did those weird 'bop-bop-bop' noises. Very strange.

Obviously, being pretty astute, we worked out who the pesky hoomans were referring to when they squawked at us.

Babs with the white legring referred to my bravest sister. Always first out of the coop, always on watch and alerting us to danger. Babs is the sister we have to obey, or else!

Cornflake has a black legring. She's always trying to wind Babs up. A peck here, a feather pluck there, she's even tried to big it up with Babs by raising her hackles and trying to stand above her. She is soon chased off though, silly sausage.

Actually, the orange legring quite matches my colouring. Colour co-ordinated. Well done hooman. Not so sure about being referred to as Ginge though.

Chilli has a blue legring. She tries to stay out of the chook politics, obviously thinks she is too cool to mix with us.

Then there is Lagatha with a yellow leg ring. Not sure why the hoomans laugh at her label name. She looks nothing like a brave Viking. In fact, I think she has some sort of problem. The slightest brush past her and she's off squawking around the place, screaming as if she's being attacked by a flock of hoomans.

The hoomans finished clucking around us and went off back into the brick-brown block. I stretched my wings out. There seemed to be a bit of roomy space here so I thought maybe, I might just have a little look around. There was the ramp going up to the coop. Underneath the coop was the safe area where those pesky hoomans struggled to reach us. There was an opening going into another area. Babs was gone, through the opening. I heard food pecking! Food! I ran in there as quick as my legs could waddle. I wasn't mistaken, there in front of my very eyes was another hanging food fountain. Nom, nom, nom. I was straight in there with Babs and we were soon joined by Cornflake and Chilli. Lagatha tried to get in but there was no space so she had to be told. Off she screamed.

I wandered around the new world. There were some interesting objects and strange contraptions. A hanging round, big leafed ball that tasted gorgeous. Various perches and a strange multi-coloured thing attached to the wall that made a pinging sound when I pecked it. There was a massive bowl area filled with loose soil. Jumping in, I was able to settle down for a luxurious bath. Scratching at the bottom, flicking earth over my back and flopping onto my sides got bits of soil into all my nooks and crannies between my feathers. Bliss! Well it was, until Babs hopped over and decided to painfully pluck out some feathers. What The Cluck!

CHAPTER 4

A STRANGE NEW WORLD

It was then that we noticed. At one end of the new area was a silver, webbed, mesh wall. On the other side of the wall were strangers! There was a big, big, grey chook, a black chook and a brown chook with black, smudgy dots all over her. They were grumbling, menacingly at us. Babs decided to go over and investigate and the big, big, grey girl hoisted up her feather bloomers, stretched her neck and ruffled her pointy, puffy, hackle feathers. Babs copied her and tried to look bigger but it was not going to happen, she was nowhere near as big. I think that made Babs a bit angry so she started squawking and pecking at the big, big, grey girl through the wall. Oh my goodness – all hell broke loose! There was awful pecking going on through that mesh wall but eventually, Babs backed off. The three girls on the other side of the wall continued to pace up and down and grumble at us though. They did not look very friendly at all. I got out of there and back into the safe area.

The soft, green floor was just lovely to walk on and explore. So much to scratch and investigate. I found quite a variety of juicy beetles and succulent bugs. Finding a delicious, mouth-watering worm was just the best, especially if I could run off and gobble it down before it was noticed by my sisters. The grey ceiling-sky was strange. Sometimes it wasn't grey but blue with white balls. Sometimes a bright yellow, round ball was up there. If I stood underneath the shining yellow ball, it's light gave me a beautiful, warm feeling. Flopping on the floor under that yellow ball was so relaxing. I could spread my legs out, extend my wings and just close my eyes for a bit enjoying the quiet, calm and soothing feelings. Bliss. Maybe this world would be okay.

Babs started getting quite bossy in this new world. She had to be in charge and, only if she allowed it, could we peck at the food or take a drink. It was best to keep out of her way or sneak a bit of food and run. Even Cornflake could be an overbearing bossy-boots. She would often peck us on the head or try to chase the rest of us away from the hanging yummy food. Occasionally, the hoomans would visit us with something extra scrummy like a roll of corn or a big branch of cabbage. I had to get in there quickly to get some before being chased off by Babs or Cornflake. I could push Chilli and Lagatha out of the way though I managed to get a decent share.

Lagatha was a strange one. Most of her feathers were gone and she was pretty much naked with pink, bobbly skin and flushed, rosy patches all over her. A few feather pins were growing out of her back but the ends looked fluffy and delicious and Babs or Cornflake, (or sometimes me – oops) would pluck them out for a delicious treat. I'm not sure why Lagatha screamed a lot – she was a strange one.

It was a bit hit and miss when those pesky hoomans came out of the big brick-brown box though. Mostly, they would come to visit with scrumptious food. Doing those weird 'bop-bop-bop' noises, they liked to squawk away about nonsense such as 'yummy eggs', 'being nice to each other' and strangely, they loved checking out our poop.

A few days after moving to our new world the pesky hoomans came out with lots of bottles and strange looking sprays in their hands. No food! They came into our coop-run area through the 'door that we must never go through' and set up a four legged long, wide perch they called a 'table'. They put the bottles and bits and bobs on the table and put some strange, white, plastic coverings over their hand-claws. They called these 'gloves' and they made a strange pinging sound as they put them on. They picked up Cornflake and held her tightly on the table, not allowing her to flap and escape. They dropped some liquid on her neck and held her in a strange almost upside down, position whilst they looked at her feet. They then put some cream on the end of one of their claws. After this, and, … I cannot believe that I am detailing this…. they lifted up her tail feathers and put one of their gloved claws into her bum! What The Cluck! Cornflake was not happy. She screamed and squawked and fought hard to get away. She managed to escape. Good for her (or they may have put her down on the floor, I'm not sure).

They tried to pick me up but I was having none of that so I got out of there and ran to the safe place under the coop. They managed to pick up Lagatha. Poor Lagatha, she was so scared and screamed non-stop throughout the disgraceful assault. The pesky hoomans also sprayed some purple colouring all over her pink, naked skin areas. How disgusting!

I stayed hidden in the corner of the safe area. Then, would you believe it, the cage wall that I was huddled against came away. Hooman hands grabbed me and pulled me out to the side of the safe area under the coop. I was caught and I could not escape. The pesky hooman took me over to the four-legged, torture table. I didn't really feel the drops going onto my neck but that gloved claw going into my bum…. I screamed to get the clucking claw out of me but the pesky hooman didn't listen (or chose to ignore me). They sprayed me with some of that horrible purple stuff and it went everywhere. I had a purple patch on my head, a purple bottom and one purple foot. Ridiculous! The pesky hooman put me down on the floor and I got out of there. I went straight back to the safe under coop area where thankfully, the cage wall had returned.

The purple stuff was disgusting and as it covered Lagatha's new fluffy feather buds, we couldn't pop them out anymore. Pesky hoomans interfering!

There had been quite a few dark nightimes and coop sleeps when the pesky hoomans squawked that we could go outside of our coop run area. I had been eyeing up the outside of the coop run. Inside, our luscious, soft, green floor had changed to dark, soggy, clumpy brown soil but just outside the 'door we must not go through', just out of my reach was other gorgeous, soft green floor.

The hoomans came over and opened the 'door that we must not go through' and, stupid, pesky hoomans, they left it wide open. We were able to escape. We were out of there like a shot. Wow ... outside of our area the luscious, soft, green floor was everywhere. There were so many mouth-watering worms, juicy bugs and scrumptious beetles to scratch around for. We all came out of our area and explored this new, luxurious, lush paradise. The pesky hoomans either didn't notice us scrambling around this new place or they couldn't catch us. We had a lovely time wandering, exploring and scavenging.

Whilst in the paradise area a few mini hoomans came out of the big brick-brownish box. They came running over towards us and one of them tried to catch me. I was having none of that so I quickly ran out of their reach. One of the mini hoomans wearing black-rimmed, glass frames over their eyes had run around to the front of me and managed to grab me quite unceremoniously, catching one of my wings awkwardly. I screeched just to let them know it might have hurt (it didn't), but a big hooman came running over shouting at the mini hooman. "Mikey, put her down, you'll hurt her" it squawked. They then told 'Mikey' and 'Molly' (this must have been the mini hoomans labels) that they would "show you both how to hold them properly". The big hooman then took me out of the little one's hands and moved me about, up and down, restricting my wings and pointing to various parts of my body labelling me with odd words. "This is the comb, this is the wattle" it said pointing to parts of my head. I just missed his fingers, I'm sure they would have made lovely worm-tasting morsels. He went on to point at various areas stating 'wing', 'leg', 'claws', 'tail' and .. What The Cluck! He lifted up my tail and they all stared at what it called the 'vent where eggs pop out'. The big hooman then handed me over to Mikey and he took me under his arm and held me tightly restricting my movements. I was stuck there. Mikey started stroking me under my beak and told me about how we were going to be best 'friends', whatever that was. I looked over and noticed Molly doing the same with Lagatha who was not happy about it and had managed to free a wing that she was flapping furiously in an effort to escape. Mikey finally put me down on the ground. I was about to get out of there when he pulled some delicious seed treats out of his pocket and held his hand out to me. Well, I thought that was probably worth a look so I waddled back towards him and pecked those seed treats right out of his grasp.

All of the hoomans must have suddenly realised we were outside the 'door we must never go through'. They blocked our way from going further in to the paradise area and ushered us back into our coop run area. Well, none of us were happy about that and we told them pesky hoomans with lots of clucking grumbling and complaining.

Those three big girls next door to our coop run area continued to pace and grumble and strut their stuff in front of us. The pesky hoomans went in their area sometimes and we soon learned that their label-names were Daisy (the big, big grey girl), Dolly (brown with black dots) and Betty (black feathers all over). We all knew that they couldn't actually get into our coop run area so whenever we were near them, a bit of a challenge was good fun. Babs used every opportunity to 'have a go', raise her heckle feathers and challenge Daisy. We would sometimes get behind Babs and squawk at those three, clucking laughing that they couldn't get to us. They didn't seem to find it amusing and would moan and complain with threatening grumbles.

CHAPTER 5

SETTLING

We settled into a routine on most days. Slowly waking as the streams of daylight seeped into the darkened coop. A poop. A bit of a preen and stretch before the going down into the coop run where Mikey or Molly had filled the breakfast food bowl. Occasionally they were late so we had to loudly let them know that they were failing in their duties. A poop. A bit of a scramble for the best bits of the food, usually ending with a nip and a peck to my head from Babs – such a bully. So a bit of a peck of Lagatha's head and she would soon screech out of the way. A scratch around to find any tasty bugs who had trespassed into our coop run overnight. Usually by this time I would start having a tummy ache that was sometimes quite painful causing me to screech a bit. I found that by going back up into the snuggly side of the coop and having a real big poop it would usually get better. Always had a bit of a sing song after that. What a relief.

The pesky hoomans would usually come out and were always interested in the big poops in the coop nest area, taking away the oval shaped, strange coloured poops. They often squawked something about how 'messy' the coop was and questioned whether we had been 'partying all night?' They would generally then open up the 'door that we should not go through' and we always managed to escape out into the lush, green paradise. Stupid hoomans. Nearly every day, the mini hooman with the Mikey' label visited with treats. He didn't mind ensuring that I was the first to peck up those gorgeous, stripey seeds so I didn't mind him picking me up from the ground to stroke my neck. I thought it best to keep him on side just to ensure I always had the first pickings. It could also be a bit scary out there in the paradise area because the caw-caw things and other flying creatures could get to us but Babs soon saw them off if they came too close and I found that if I stayed behind Mikey as much as possible, I was quite safe.

I was enjoying a good scratch around one morning when I heard a strange but familiar grumbling sound behind me. I turned around and found myself facing Daisy! There was no metal, mesh wall between us and she was cackling menacingly at me. I tried to get as far away from her as possible but she was too fast and too strong. She launched herself at me and took hold of my comb in her beak. I struggled but she would not let go. She kicked me hard with her foot, catching one of her sharp pointed claws in my wing. Suddenly,

Babs was there. She jumped at Daisy screaming and squawking giving me time to get out of there. I didn't look back but I heard the fighting continuing and a pesky hooman shouting at both Daisy and Babs to "stop it".

When I was far enough away, I turned around and saw a hooman in between Daisy and Babs with a big bristly, brush contraption. The pesky hooman was blocking them both from getting at each other. Over Daisy's wing I spotted Dolly and Betty deviously trying to creep around the hooman to get near to Cornflake and Chilli who were standing watching the commotion. The pesky hooman stopped them in their tracks and they went back to the other end of the lush, green paradise area. With Cornflake, Chilli, Babs and Lagatha, who had suddenly appeared behind me, I went back into our area into the safe under coop den. I checked myself over. A bit of rearranging of my feathers and cleaning out of the dirt left behind by Daisy's spiteful attack and I felt a bit okay again. Cornflake noticed some red water on my head and pecked at me. I squawked at her and got out of there. It did feel a bit sore but the red water soon stopped running down my face. That was not a good day.

After the next dark time and coop sleep the hoomans left the 'door we must not go through' open again. We were ready for the other girls this time and we kept well out of Daisy, Dolly and Betty's way. The pesky hoomans were always around with that bristle, brush thing but we all tended to keep to our own sides of the paradise area. A couple of times Babs and Daisy got a bit too close to each other and ruffled themselves up trying to intimidate each other. The hooman would usually get in between them but mostly Babs would turn around and come back to us.

One day I was busy scratching at some roots, (they seemed to go up towards a big bush with large, red flowers climbing up the wall but I wasn't interested in them so I kicked them out of the way). I looked around and that Betty was next to me scratching one of the last soft, green areas on the floor. She noticed me. I spotted her. She would have to be warned to keep away. Then I saw a pink, juicy worm. Yummy.

Another time out in the paradise area, I found myself next to Dolly. She reminded me a bit of Lagatha because she was soon running off screaming. All I did was give her a quick head peck as I could have sworn that I saw a tiny bug moving in there.

We came out of our area one morning and noticed that the ceiling-sky was very grey and dark. There was a lot of blowing about going on and the bushes and trees were bending forwards and backwards and looked like they were going to fall over. Water started coming out of the ceiling-sky, there was a startling flash of bright, white light and then a booming, loud, crashing bang above us. The hoomans came running towards us and ushered us back into our coop run area. I was straight under the coop into the safe den area. The ceiling water couldn't get us in there so we all huddled together. It was quite scary and it went on for a long time before the blowing and the ceiling-sky water stopped. When we came out of the den area, I noticed that it was wet, squelchy and slimy everywhere. There was water all over the floor and lots of big round, squishy puddles – that water tasted good, much better than the water in the troughs.

One day I went into our coop after Lagatha and Chilli and snuggled into them as usual but when I went to move it felt much tighter than usual. I moved to the other side of the coop and settled into a big grey bundle of snuggly feathers. When the light came into the coop in the morning Daisy pushed me out of the way to get to the door. I followed Babs, Cornflake and Dolly down the ramp to the hanging food. Something was a bit different this morning but I couldn't quite put my claw on it. Hmmm. Anyway food …. Yummy.

Going into the other part of our area through the big opening I noticed that the metal, mesh wall was gone. Those three strange chooks were not over in that area either. I'm not sure where they had gone, but I went through to the new area and explored. Babs and Betty came in as well and we all scratched around together. I'm sure something was a bit different but I just couldn't quite work out what it was. Then I noticed a new hanging food bowl. Food…… Yummy.

I quite liked this new world. I had all my sisters with me, the pesky hoomans performed their duties pretty well and made sure that our coop run area was regularly cleaned of poop and they kept our hanging food bowls and water troughs replenished. On occasion, we needed to loudly squawk and remind them but generally, they performed well. Often, (though not often enough for my liking) they provided hanging cabbage branches or rolls of corn. Sometimes the cabbage branches were hung up a little too high and those pesky hoomans did a lot of squawking and laughing when we jumped for them. Strange! Mikey was a bit of a bonus, bringing us treats that I was always offered first.

Most times we were able to go out via the 'door that you must never go through'. Daisy continued to look out for danger and warn us of anything coming too near. Babs still tried to peck at Daisy but she knew who was the boss. Lagatha and Dolly continued to run around the world screaming if anyone went too near to them. I still had some grumbling stomach aches and big poops but this didn't happen as much as it did when I was in the former brown world home. And when I had a particularly big round poop I sang the loudest, happiest, clucking song ever that had ever been squawked in the world.

The pesky hoomans came out of the big brownish box one morning with rolls of green bendy mesh. They spent a long time putting it all over our cage area and after that they stopped leaving the 'door you must never go through' open. The bottom of their legs started to smell strange when they came into our coop run area and as well as the usual, stupid 'bop-bop-bop' noises they did, they squawked about 'flockdown' and 'flu', whatever that was. It did not matter how much we all grumbled and clucking moaned about the 'door you must never go through', they would not leave it open anymore. They would need some more training.

I was sat on one of the perches in our area, having a doze, when I spotted movement out of the corner of one of my eyes. I stared down at the ground and there was a small, grey, furry creature scratching on the floor eating up bits of corn that I had overlooked. I flew down from that perch faster than a pesky hooman running when the falling ceiling water came. I trapped the creature under my foot and curled my claws around the wriggling body. I pecked the head and it stopped wriggling and felt limp. Betty spotted it and came my way. I got out of there as fast as a caw-caw swooping across the ceiling-sky. As I dashed through to the other side of the coop run area Cornflake noticed the creature flopping out of my beak and she came after me. That caused everyone to look up and over ran Daisy and Babs. Well, I was not about to give up my prize easily. Babs managed to grab a leg in her beak and started pulling at it. Wow, the furry creature could stretch really long and really thin. Babs pulled away and stringy bits fell out of the middle of the creature. Daisy soon had those. I managed to run off with the head in my beak and gobbled it down before Babs caught up. That was a lovely treat .... Yummy.

One morning I noticed that Betty wasn't her usual nervous and fearful self. When we came down for our morning food, she stayed in the nesting area in the coop. She didn't come down to explore the new bugs and worms that had ventured into our coop run over night. She didn't even come down when the pesky hoomans hung up a new cabbage branch. We all took it in turns to go up and check on Betty. I gave her a little preen and snuggled into her for a while. After a while her eyes closed and she stopped moving about. She must have been settled and comfortable although, she wasn't quite as cosy and warm as usual. I went down the ramp, it was time for an afternoon snack and one of the pesky hoomans came into the coop run. They reached into our coop nest and carried Betty out. She wasn't struggling or screaming or trying to escape. That was not like Betty. The hoomans took her out of our coop run area and took her into the big, brick-brown box. We took it in turns to keep going up into the coop to see if they had returned her but the coop nest remained empty with just a big dip in the straw bed where Betty had previously sat. She didn't come back.

CHAPTER 6

A NEW SEASON

The dark times started to be shorter. The bright, yellow circle in the ceiling-sky started to feel warm again. The hoomans started coming out from the big brownish box a bit more often and the world started to change again. Every morning when I came down the ramp with my sisters there were hoomans in the lush (now brown) paradise area doing all sorts of things, scratching the floor with big metal shovels, banging in wooden walls and putting white and brown colours on the outside of the brownish box. They regularly did their 'bop-bop-bop' noises and squawked about 'having a Spring clean' and 'flockdown' soon being over.

I came down after Daisy and Babs and Cornflake one morning to find the mini hoomans running around outside our coop run. They were kicking a big white round ball thing to each other. What The Cluck! It crashed with an almighty 'bang' on the door. Well I screeched and flew out of there, heading straight for the safe under coop area. Those pesky hoomans. They made such a racket, screeching and shouting and gaggling away. A big hooman shouted at them and they ran into the big brownish box. Thank goodness for that – some peace and quiet. Time to get on with my scratching. A worm popped it's head out of the dark, rich soil. 'Got you'. I pulled that out of the ground and ran off to the corner to munch on my prize. I looked around and none of my sisters had noticed. They were all crowded around the 'door we must not go through'. I gobbled down that wriggly, meaty worm – yummy – and ran over to investigate. The door was slightly open. I pushed into Daisy, who pushed into Cornflake and it opened wider. Haha, escape. We were out of there.

What a lovely afternoon. The yellow ball in the sky was warm. Standing just near the big brown side wall of the paradise area I could spread my wings and feel the balmy heat warming me. A little explore behind the coop run and I found a large, dusty, rectangular area with little green shoots sprouting everywhere. I scratched and pecked them out of the way and dug down to form a nice cosy, hollow bed. Perfect for a bath. I kicked up the crumbly, sandy soil and covered every nook and cranny between my feathers and spikey plumes. It was bliss!

The ceiling started to darken a bit and wouldn't you know it, those pesky hoomans came out of that big brownish box to ruin our fun. They came over towards us, not with bowls of scrumptious treats but with grumpy, sour faces that I'm sure I had never seen before. They picked up Lagatha and lifted her through the door back into the coop run. Another hooman came over and picked up Babs and in she went.

I got out of there and managed to run back into the coop run area. I watched as they picked up my sisters one by one and put them back into our coop run. I squeezed myself into the corner but then noticed the door still open. I quietly and gently ran out back around to my bathing pod.

Lagatha and Cornflake were running around behind the coop run screaming at the hoomans to come catch them. I heard the hoomans shouting 'this is the last two, you go that way, I'll go this way'. I heard Lagatha and Cornflake squawking at those pesky hoomans so they must have been caught. I thought I'd better get out of there before they caught me too. I ran towards one of the bigger bushes behind the coop run. I hopped underneath and up onto a branch and sat quietly so as not to be noticed by those pesky hoomans. I could hear Lagatha screaming and scrabbling to get back out of the door but no chance – it was banged shut with a loud clang. The hoomans walked off back to the big brownish box. It all went quiet. Apart from the grumbling and clucking moaning from my sisters.

There were a couple of chirping sounds above me, high up in the bush and I spotted the shadow of a caw-caw creature gliding high overhead. I looked around the paradise area. It felt bigger, vast and empty without my sisters running around. I zoomed in on an area near the big brownish box where a small patch of tall, green, pointy foliage was gently wafting to and fro in the breeze. Food! Yummy. I jumped off that branch and waddled over, passing my sisters trapped inside the coop run. They saw where I was heading and were not amused that they were going to miss out. I held my head high and gave a little clucking mutter as I passed. Mmmm, it would be all mine.

The foliage was lovely and soft and tasty. A bit of a scratch around the bottom and, yummy, bugs popped out. I soon gobbled them up. I noticed movement just to the side of my foot. An extra-long, fat, juicy, pink, worm, yummy. I scratched around some more and found a tube of root sticking out. I tried that but it wasn't too good. A bit more scratching and before I knew it I had moved around to another side of the big brownish box. I spotted a few flying bugs near an opening in a wooden wall joined onto the side of the brownish box. I was straight over there. Gulp. Caught one of them. Yummy. Another flying bug flew out through the opening. I chased it through the gap and found myself in another lush, green paradise. I soon forgot the flying bug and started to scratch around on the lovely, soft, glorious, green floor. I encountered a few brightly coloured and quite smelly plants but they were just in the way of my scratching so I hooked them out of the way. Scratching and prodding, digging and breaking up the floor with no interruptions was amazing.

I noticed that the ceiling overhead was starting to grow even darker just as a pesky hooman wandered into my blissful paradise. I realised they were coming for me just a little too late and the hooman scooped me up and held me tightly under one of their thin wing side arms. The hooman was squawking about how I'd "got out" and they were going to "take me back to the neighbour". As the hooman was pointing to the big brownish box, I managed to scrabble out from under their thin arm and flap off into another bush. I scrambled under the bush and through the undergrowth, pushing the low hanging plants out of the way as I ran out of reach of the pesky hooman. I ran and ran until I reached a small clearing. There was no lush green flooring here, just brown, muddy earth covered in broken down plant litter and debris. All around the edge of the clearing were gigantic trees stretching up to darkening, midnight blue, ceiling-sky. There were various, odd shaped perches sprouting out from the centre of the trees covered in small, various shaped greeneries. How strange. High up above me there appeared to be lots of activity and noise. After a bit more scratching on the floor, a few more tasty bug and worm morsels I began feeling tired so I decided to hop up onto one of the perches for a doze. I hopped from one perch to another until I found the most perfect, steady and stable perch. I secured my feet, snuggled down and drifted off with a gentle purr.

A sudden jolt startled me awake. The world had turned a dark, murky, gloomy shade of blackened grey. Beams of narrow light shone through the top of the tree canopy illuminating my perch. Towards the end of the perch was a … What The Cluck was that! There was a huge, feathered, bright white with black smudgy markings, creature with large, round eyes just squatting on large taloned feet, inquisitively staring at me. It turned its large head to the side and made a strange 'twooo' sound. Somewhere in the distance an echoing 'twit' sound responded. The creature returned it's 'twooo' noise and before long a cacophony of twitting and twooing was booming around the darkness. The bizarre creature then spread out it's vast, feathery wings and launched itself off the perch, disappearing off into the night with a fluttering whoosh.

I suddenly noticed the various sounds echoing around me. Strange screeching noises in the distance pierced the rustling sound of the wafting greeneries. I could make out snuffling, scratching sounds down on the ground but I couldn't see anything down there. The screeching sound grew louder and was followed by a yelping noise nearby. I moved closer into the centre of the tree and crouched down as low as I could on the perch. I tucked my head under my wing. I couldn't see anything now so obviously nothing could see me. A clawing, scraping noise coincided with a vibration travelling up the tree reverberating through the bark. I peeked out from under my wing and looked down. What The Cluck was that? A russet red, slender creature with a long snout and white bib was on two legs leaning against the tree. It was using it's forearms to scratch and tear at the bark. Those claws looked pretty sharp. It raised its snout up towards me and sniffed the air, drawing back it's lips exposing razor-sharp, pointy, creamy white teeth. Something darted off from the back of the tree into the low hanging bushes and plants that I had travelled through earlier. The creature jerked it's head around towards the swishing rustle of the bush and lowered itself down to the ground, crouching on all four limbs it soundlessly crept towards the undergrowth. Suddenly, it jumped up and launched itself on all four legs into the scrub, with just the white tip of its big bushy tail detectable in the dark brown and khaki green vegetation. And then it was gone. A gentle, rustling noise softly resonated on the breeze as the creature disappeared into the darkness grew until not a sound could be heard. Being quite astute, I surmised that the creature was not one I'd like to meet again in a hurry. I thought it best to hunker down and go back to being hidden under my wing. I snuggled in and closed both eyes slowly dozing off to the strange sounds in the trees.

I woke to all sorts of strange flying creatures coming and going into and out of my tree. The noise was deafening and some of the small feathered creatures were squabbling loudly and nastily pecking at each other. It was time to get out of there. I hopped from perch to perch back down the tree to the ground and waddled over to the open, clearing. The morning dew had softened the ground and the earth under my feet crumbled and broke down as I walked. Perfect for scratching.

I was happily scrambling around in the rich, dark soil that was presenting me with a bounty of small bugs and beetles when I heard pesky hooman shouting behind me. I recognised Mikey's call as he shouted my name. Seed treats! Yummy. I ran quickly towards the sound of his voice and spotted him peering under the low hanging plants that bordered the clearing. As I reached him he scooped me up into his arms and positioned me so my wings were held tightly around me. He was stroking my neck feathers and shouting to the big hooman that he had 'found me'. Stupid mini hooman. I had 'found' him and where were my treats? Taken back through the opening into the paradise area and put back into the coop run, my sisters ran over to investigate the clumps of soil on my feet still crumbling off in tiny pieces. I looked up expectantly at Mikey, clucking my disgust that he had failed to provide me with my treats when he threw down some delicious seeds. Quite generously I thought, I decided to excuse the delay.

A few days later the big hoomans came out of the brick-brownish box and started moving all of the green netting. The 'door you must not go through' was left open again regularly and we could spend most of the light time scratching around in the paradise area.

CHAPTER 7

A BAD DAY

It started as a beautiful, warm, chilled out day. The big hoomans had come and fed us our food as required, they had cleaned our coop and coop run and opened the 'door you must not go through' as usual. They had returned to their big brick-brownish box and left us to our scratching. Daisy and Babs must have sensed something was amiss, they seemed to be on alert more than usual and were patrolling the boundaries of the paradise area, ignoring the rich, bug infested earth.

Without warning, a huge, russet coloured creature, similar to the creature I had spotted from the escape tree, zoomed through the paradise area towards Lagatha. Razor sharp, pointed, creamy-white teeth grabbed her neck, enveloped her head and ripped it off with a snarl and a penetrating, ferocious growl. Lagatha dropped to the ground. Red, thick water surged out of her exposed, ravaged, neck stump, spraying over the now scarlet, drenched soil. Ear-splitting squawks pierced the tranquil quiet as we all screamed and ran haphazardly around the paradise area.

Daisy, brave and courageous Daisy, actually ran towards the murderous, sneering creature who had turned and set it's sight on Babs. I bumped into Dolly as I tried to remember the way back to the coop run. I flapped my wings to try and jump over her but she was running around in circles and I landed on her back causing us both to tumble over. I saw the creature run towards us leaving Daisy behind lying limp and lifeless on the floor her head at an odd angle with a gaping hole under her beak that was pumping more red liquid into the ground.

I spotted the 'door you must not go through' and ran speedily towards it using my flapping wings to propel me forward. I managed to run through the door and sprinted under the coop to the safe area. Dolly was still running around in circles and actually bumped into the deadly, viscous creature. It opened its wide jaws and bit down on her back causing her to scream unnaturally and roll over out of the creature's path. Chilli was cowering in the corner of the paradise area and the homicidal creature ran past her heading for Babs again. Babs flapped her wings and darted one way and then another, trying to evade the monster but it was too fast and too agile. It launched itself onto Babs holding her down with it's front legs and picked her up by snapping it's long mouth around her neck and lifting her off of the ground. She went limp but it kept hold of her dangling, flaccid, hanging body.

A booming, clanging noise erupted as the big hoomans came running out of the brick-brownish box holding silver pots that they were banging with wooden sticks causing crashing, thumping, clattering sounds. The fiendish, jagged-toothed creature leapt up onto the wall and disappeared over the top with Babs still dangling from its jaws. The hoomans screamed (what were obviously obscenities), running towards the wall continuing to make the loud, clanging, bangings from the pots that they were holding. They stopped shouting and cursing as the creature disappeared over the wall and it was gone in a flash. All was suddenly very quiet.

I peered out from under the coop area and looked at the macabre scene in the paradise area. Babs was gone. Daisy lay motionless on the ground in the middle of a huge, scarlet stained circle on the ground. Lagatha, I think it was Lagatha, lay on the ground. Her neck flopped onto the side with entrails protruding and still seeping thick, crimson water onto her wing feathers. A tiny, shrivelled ball that looked strangely like a beak with feathers was lying nearby. Dolly was gently squawking and trying to stand but she was struggling. She used her outstretched wings to try to push herself up from the ground but she kept tumbling forward.

I spotted Chilli, still quivering in the corner of the paradise area, hunched up into a small ball of russet brown and cream feathers. I heard a noise behind me. Cornflake popped her head out of the coop above me, at the top of the ramp. She looked startled and anxious and quickly retreated back into the dark coop disappearing from sight. I manoeuvred myself back under the coop, finding a dark corner where I could preen and check my feathers. I heard a strange, wailing noise. I peeked through the cage side wall and noticed one of the hoomans gently holding Dolly who was not struggling to get away. The hooman had lots of water coming out of their eyes and was speaking softly to Dolly who seemed quite lethargic and sleepy. The hooman took her up towards, and into the brick-brownish box. I never saw Dolly again.

The other big hooman picked up Chilli and brought her into the coop-run. He looked at her all over. He looked at her feet, checked under her wings and turned her around in his arms. He told her that she was 'okay'. He spotted me under the coop and called my name telling me to come out. What The Cluck! Did the pesky hooman really expect me to give up my safe, dark corner and venture out to where that monster might be. The little hooman Mikey came into the coop run and called my name, inviting me to come out from under the coop. He was holding out his hand and I spotted some yummy grey sunflower hearts.

Hhhmmm food. I was still unsure it was safe but then I spotted Cornflake bounding and fluttering down the ramp and she ran over towards Mikey's outstretched hand. Well, I was not going to miss out on that so I ran over as well. Those sunflower hearts sure did taste good.

The coop was strangely quiet that night. It didn't feel quite as warm or snuggly without my sisters. I am sure that I kept seeing flashes of russet brown fur out of the side of my eyes. I kept imaging the fountains of thick, red water and the squawks of fear and pain that came from my missing sisters replayed over and over in my mind. What would we do without Babs and Daisy to look out for us? I already missed Dolly and Lagatha's squeals when I brushed past them to get comfortable. I snuggled in between Cornflake and Chilli and settled down to doze. Just the one eye closed tonight though.

CHAPTER 8

THE INTERLOPERS

It was very quiet in the coop run. Cornflake bossed us about a bit when it came to food time but we always seemed to have plenty. Chilli was not her usual, bouncy self and waddled around with her head and tail held low. There was no queue for the dirt bath and it stayed pretty empty on the coop at nights. Those pesky hoomans stopped forgetting to close the 'door that we must not go through' so we couldn't get out into the paradise area. Although, for some reason I felt a bit scared too scared to go out there.

One morning I came down to an almighty fracas going on in the paradise area. Cocking my head to get a good look I spotted Mikey and another mini hooman carrying some brown boxes. The big hoomans were stood over them. They were telling Mikey and Molly to remember to "hold them carefully". One of the big hoomans was holding a very small, odd shaped hooman that was making an ear piercing, wailing noise. The big hooman was swaying as if a soft breeze was rocking them from side to side like the branches in a big tree. The hooman was whispering and murmuring about a 'mocking bird' and about how 'it was all okay Maisy'. Cornflake, Chilli and I let it be known what we thought about all of the commotion with a few clucking, grumbling squawks.

The crowd of hoomans went around the back of our coop into the other coop run area. I made my way over to enter the area and keep an eye on what was going on but a big barrier of metal, holey wire had been put across the opening. What The Cluck was going on? Cornflake pushed me out of the way to get a better look. As we watched, Mikey and Molly opened the brown boxes and lifted some strange girls out, placing them on the floor under a new coop that had been added into the area. Four chooks were put into our extended coop run and given lots of fresh yummy food to munch on. The hoomans left the coop run area leaving those four interlopers staring at us with their beady, sneaky eyes. Cornflake gave a grumbling, deep warning squawk. They knew not to come too near to our coop run. They didn't seem too interested in the yummy food left for them and one by one they disappeared up into the new coop. Cornflake patrolled the barriered, opening for most of the rest of the light time but they didn't come back down again.

Coming down the next morning I went straight for breakfast. Mikey had obviously been in and filled our food bowls. Well done Mikey, his training was going well. I enjoyed a bit of fresh water that, no matter how hard I tried, I could never get as tasty and dirty as a puddle, when I heard a strange noise coming from the extended coop run area. I waddled over to go in through the opening and spotted those four interlopers. Cornflake came up besides me and stood at the barrier opening. One of those strange girls came right up to her and raised herself up, fluffing out her hackles and stretching her neck. Cornflake was having none of that so did the same before pecking at her through the holes in the barrier. The strange girl tried to peck back but she was nowhere near as fast as Cornflake, who jumped back before resuming her tall, big, fluffing up stance. The altercation was abruptly stopped by a big hooman who came up behind the strange girl and lifted her off the ground. She let out an almighty shriek as the hooman put a green ring on her leg. "There you go Hetty" he yelled over the exaggerated cries of pain.

We watched as the big hooman put a red ring on 'Clementine', a white ring on 'Chucky' and a yellow ring on 'Charlotte'.

The hooman then went into the extended coop run area with ... the torture table and various bottles and jars. I got out of there as quick as possible. There was no way I wanted to be anywhere near where hooman fingers investigated and inserted creams and lotions in delicate areas. We heard the cries of pain that I guessed were not exaggerated this time.

Those strange girls were very odd looking. They were all pretty naked with just one or two feathers protruding at awkward angles from their skinny, pink bodies. If only we could get into their coop run area. Those feathers looked tasty and I was sure that they would pop out with little or no effort.

Our morning routine was now to have breakfast, have a big smelly poop to shake off the night, a few gulps of water and then straight over to the barrier to warn off those interlopers before my big morning tummy ache poop. The one labelled 'Hetty' was always trying to outstretch Cornflake although, she tried it with me on one occasion and I soon pecked her comb when I could reach it. She was a bit scary though, so I usually got out of there. Chilli never wanted to investigate these intruders, she just stayed behind us watching from afar. I noticed that the one labelled 'Clementine' was also not interested in coming over to the barrier preferring to stay way back under the new coop. She reminded me of a sister who used to shriek whenever I brushed past her. What was her name? I struggled to recall.

The big round yellow ball overhead started getting really, really hot again. It was actually quite nice sometimes and flopping down on the ground with my wings and legs outstretched keeping the dark, damp ground cold underneath was relaxing.

One morning as I sat relaxing in the warmth, I spotted Mikey and Molly in the paradise area. Mikey came over for a 'chat' as usual so I hurried over to catch the seed treats he was likely to have. But there were none! Instead, he unlocked the 'door that we must never go through' and left it wide open. Woo hoo, escape. Although, for some reason I felt a bit too scared to go through. I scratched around the doorway not going out into the paradise area, despite spotting some luscious new green shoots at the side of the area. The big hoomans had come out of the big brick-brownish block to join Mikey and Molly and the strange blob thing Maisy was with them. "Come on Ginge" Mikey called out. He held his hand out but being quite astute I was fully aware that he had no seed treats in there. Cornflake brushed past me and boldly waddled out into the paradise area. She headed straight for those fresh, luscious shoots that I had spotted earlier. Well I was not having that so I ran head first, straight over to the treasure and gobbled them up. I scratched around next to where the shoots had been and found a gorgeous, juicy, pink worm. Yummy.

We had been out in the paradise area for a while when I spotted Mikey lying down on the floor. He was staring up at the blue ceiling watching the white fluffy balls drifting slowly overhead. I wandered over to check on whether his hand might have some seed treats but disappointingly there were none there. He was quite warm and a bit snuggly so I climbed up on him and settled down to enjoy the warmth coming from the big yellow circle. I shut just one eye, it was soo relaxing. I felt Mikey scratching under my beak. It felt a bit like being preened, it was quite comforting actually. I listened as Mikey told me about how he was "only eating vegetables from now on" and how "meat" (whatever that is) was cruel. He told me about how animals used to be chased by cave people a long time ago and how the cave people would shout at them yelling "Me Eat You". He explained that this was how the flesh of animals came to be known as 'meat'. What The Cluck! I was not totally sure about what he was saying but eating flesh did not sound good. I was up and out of there, but not before leaving Mikey with a bit of a smelly poop.

Our routine soon changed again and Mikey or Molly would come and open the 'door that we must not go through' after every breakfast time. There were always pesky hoomans in the paradise area though who would often interrupt me by blocking my way when I found a particularly tasty root or shrub to peck at. What a cheek. More training needed.

One of those days in the paradise area I was happily scratching at a bit of the ground having found a lovely, long root that seemed to go on for ever and ever, well until it came out of the ground and went up to some big tree shrub thing growing up the side of the brick brownish box with big, red smelly leaves growing out of the branches. The pesky hoomans were not watching so I managed to pull out a few of those tasty tubers and gobble them down. Suddenly I heard a low, throaty, grumbling sound behind me. I turned and found myself facing the interloper with the 'Hetty' label. She towered over me, blocking out the light from the big, yellow ball overhead. Slowly moving behind her was the one with the 'Chucky' label. I looked around for help but Cornflake and Chilli were nowhere to be seen. There was some kind of commotion involving some of the other interlopers, going on in the far corner of the paradise area and the hoomans were completely focused on the action. I made a quick dash to go around Hetty but Chucky blocked my way. As I turned to make a dash for it the other way Hetty jumped up onto my back, using her thick, sharp claws to hook into my back. A searing, stabbing, hot pain spread through my body. I cried out with an ear-splitting, screeching shriek. The hoomans turned and spotted Hetty's brutal attack on me. They ran over and picked up both Hetty and Chucky. My legs started to feel a bit shaky so I settled down onto the ground. The pesky hoomans walked away carrying the two terrifying tormentors.

CHAPTER 9

IN A DREAMY WORLD

They disappeared into the extra coop run area but were soon lumbering back over to me. I could feel a warm stream of thick, sticky fluid flowing down my back and over my downturned tail feathers. I was feeling sleepy when one of the big hoomans lifted me up from the ground and carried me over to the brick brownish box. The world started to look hazy and vague as I rocked from side to side in the hooman's arms. Going in through a gap into the big brownish box I looked around at strange silver, shiny contraptions around the vast, sterile area. Another hooman placed a caged basket on a huge table and I was placed inside and the metal opening closed trapping me inside. There was some snuggly bedding inside and I settled down resting my head on the bottom of the basket.

I drifted in and out of sleep as I felt the world move around me. I was suddenly in a very bright area being pulled out of the basket onto a high table and faced another strange hooman in a green coat staring at me. This hooman picked me up and poked and prodded me all over. I felt a sting as the hooman pushed something into my side. I felt a nice, relaxing feeling spread through my body and the searing pain subsided. I was just beginning to feel comfortable and tranquil when What The Cluck! I felt the hooman insert something into my 'vent where eggs pop out'. It was soo uncomfortable but thankfully it was taken out again pretty quickly. Those pesky hoomans blathered on about all kinds of strange topics talking about 'medicines' and 'antibiotics' and 'fees'. I felt myself being gently placed back into the basket and finally I could settle down and drift off to sleep.

When I woke up I was in the darkened basket. It was quiet and still. Looking around I noticed a small pot containing a porridge-like substance. Food! I inched closer, my legs feeling weak and shaky but I managed to reach the pot and peck at the grainy, gloopy substance. Yum! I didn't realise just how hungry I was. I made short work of the contents of that food bowl. Attached to the cage door of the basket was another bowl with water glistening inside. A few gulps and my thirst was quenched. I struggled to stand with a few bumbling attempts. I managed to stretch my legs and stand up fully so I could eject a creamy, sticky, liquid poop. That felt so much better.

As I was turning around to look for a comfortable spot to settle back down for a nap I heard, and then saw, one of those big pesky hoomans walk towards me. With one of those stupid "bop, bop, bop" calls they opened the basket door, reached in and pulled me out quite unceremoniously. Restricting my wings and holding me tightly another pesky hooman came at me with a strange tube-shaped thing. The hooman then grabbed by beak, forced it open and squirted a thick, sticky liquid towards the back of my throat. What The Cluck! I shrieked and squawked in pain, not that it did hurt but it could have, before I was placed back into the cage basket. Obviously, a shriek could make them put them down so I decided to remember that. I managed to settle down in a cosy, comfortable spot and drifted off to sleep.

When I next woke, those pesky hoomans did the same again. All of my shrieking and squawking made no difference this time. They didn't put me back in the cage basket though. I was carried over to the coop run and put on the ground. I looked around and spotted Cornflake and Chilli. I ambled over towards them and noticed a wire barrier separating us. I tried to get through but I was blocked at every attempt. I then noticed that brutish bully 'Hetty' behind Chilli. I squawked a warning to Chilli and Cornflake who didn't seem to be too worried. They did duck down and get out of Hetty's way though allowing her to push forward to the barrier. She stared at me menacingly as she grumbled a warning to keep away. I was out of there. I turned and muttering in squawking complaints I ran over to the small coop in the run area, up the ramp and into the dark, safe confines of the small nesting area. I turned and peered out to check that she couldn't follow but as she paced backwards and forwards I spotted that she couldn't come through the barrier from the other side either.

That annoying tummy grumbling started causing me to moan some more. Thankfully, I had the dark nesting area all to myself so I settled down ready for an extra big poop deposit. Wow, this poop took a great deal of effort to push out. It stung as it passed and the relief was amazing. What a song I sang. That is one major poop I had to announce to the world. I hopped back down that ramp just as Mikey came into the coop run. He swept me up into his arms and tried to sing along with me. Poor mini hooman Mikey – he couldn't quite squawk a tune as well as I could. He gave it a try anyway. I flapped my wings to let him know it was time to place me back onto the ground and he did as told. Mikey then put his arm into the dark coop, lifted out an enormous oval shaped stone and disappeared off back into the brick-brownish box shouting something about a "giant egg".

CHAPTER 10

THE START OF A NEW CHAPTER

I noticed that the days were not staying bright for very long now and the dark times were longer. I was still able to go out into the paradise area occasionally but only when those pesky hoomans were around. The best of times were when the big yellow ball overhead was shining down and Mikey, Molly and Maisy were scratching around in the paradise area. Mikey and Molly were well trained in providing seed treats. Being quite astute, I followed them around, squawking and muttering and they would laugh and throw more seed treats down for me. If they were sitting on the ground and I hopped up onto their legs or shoulder it made them make more funny giggling noises and that would often get me another few treats. Training them was going well.

I was in the paradise area on a particularly bright, but windy morning having summoned a hooman to come and let me out, when I felt the ground moving behind me. I looked over my wing and spotted Hetty scratching the floor with her back to me. What The Cluck! There was no wire barrier between us. I'm sure that the world turned into slow motion as I watched as Hetty stood up fully, stretched her neck and slowly turned towards me. She spotted me and started lumbering over, heading my way. I squawked and ran. Turning on my claws, I ran over towards Mikey who was sat down, making a mud pie (or something similar). He realised that something was wrong and stood up. Perfect. I managed to sneak in behind his legs and this stopped Hetty in her tracks. She cocked her head to the side, obviously trying to work out if she could get to me without the mini hooman noticing. Obviously there was not a chance of that, Mikey has been well trained to protect me. Hetty turned and waddled off in an obvious huff. I squawked a goodbye with a little giggle.

Mikey sat back down to continue his mud pie making. I couldn't stand behind his legs anymore so I waddled off to the bush area for a little scratch. Would you believe it! I found Cornflake and Chilli. They were both scratching around under the big bushy leaves of a new mini tree with red ends. I mumbled a greeting and they stopped scratching and turned towards me. Woo hoo, back with my sisters. I moved in between the to investigate the ground they had been scratching. Ooh, a juicy worm. Then I spotted a tasty bit of root that I pulled at and it came out of the ground with a long trail of beetles and bugs attached. Yummy. I looked around and Chilli and Cornflake had wandered off. What The Cluck! So much for our great reunion.

I decided to carry on scratching and managed to find some wonderful treats just as I noticed I was accompanied by the sister with the name label Clementine. I pecked at her neck just to let her know the best bugs were mine, she understood and moved back to let me peck at the juicy, plump worm that she had just unearthed. Just as I was about to pull the whole worm out of its tiny hole in the earth the one called Chucky ran in between us and grabbed it out from under me. I managed to catch the tail end of the worm as she ran off. The worm stretched and stretched but despite all my strength I lost my grip and Chucky ran off with her prize. Well, I was not having that. I chased her. Between the leaves, over the mound of mud that Mikey had built, through some kind of flower chain that Molly had been working on, causing her to scream, leading to a big pesky hooman running over, through a raised area of fragrant, colourful mini trees, causing another big pesky hooman to run over shouting some strange, ugly sounding words. Chucky turned and I managed to grab the end of my worm that was dangling from her beak. I ran with it and it strained and extended until it popped apart. I ran over to a shaded and leafy part of the paradise area and gobbled that worm down before it could be stolen again.

Mikey came over and picked me up, restraining my wings as he secured and held me tightly. Obviously, this was the end of time out in the paradise area. He walked over to the small coop area and placed me down on the ground. Thankfully, my food bowl had been refilled. Well done hoomans. I started munching on the yummy chow as Mikey closed the small coop area door. The big hoomans carrying the mini-Maisy and

Mikey and Molly wandered off to the brick brownish box and disappeared inside.

I scratched around the ground in my small coop area just as Cornflake appeared at my side. I turned and spotted Chucky pecking at the food bowl. What The Cluck! That was my food bowl. I waddled over towards Chucky just as a shadow appeared overhead and a scary, low grumbling noise grew louder and closer. Hetty strutted through the opening that no longer had a wire barrier in place. I tried to run past her but she grabbed my comb and pulled hard causing a sharp, jolting sting. I screamed in agonising pain and managed to get away by running past her into the big coop run area. I struggled to see where I was going as a thick, gooey, red liquid dropped down over my left eye. I found the ramp that led up to the big coop and shot up there with a flap and a few hops. Inside the darkened coop I found my old corner and snuggled down for a doze.

I woke to streams of light coming through the cracks in the coop just as the door blocking our way to the ramp and the coop run area slowly opened with a purring sound. I stretched my neck and stood up to flap my wings and shake off the achy feelings I had from sitting in the corner of the coop for a long time. Chilli was perched next to me. I spotted Clementine over in the far corner. Chucky stood and pecked Clementine as she passed her and waddled towards the door but she didn't go through. She stood back and waited for Hetty who emerged from the corner at the back, to slowly wander over and position herself in the opening. She sat there for a while, peering around, obviously inspecting the coop run area before flapping down the ramp. I could hear Hetty pecking at what was obviously a freshly filled hanging feeder. Food! There seemed to be a bit of a scramble as a mass of feathers and legs and flapping wings manoeuvred into the queue for the exit. I managed to get in the queue after Chilli and waited patiently for my turn to descend into the main coop run area and access that yummy food.

We all managed to find a space around the feed and had a good breakfast. I looked up and found myself next to Hetty. I was out of there. As I ran past Hetty she pecked at my comb. I ducked down and froze in a crouching position. Hetty inspected my back with a gentle peck of approval and moved away. Phew, I knew to keep out of her way and if necessary, submit for an inspection.

The days were growing shorter. Hetty, Chucky, Charlotte, Clementine, Cornflake, Chilli and me settled into our suitable daily routine. The pesky hoomans were mostly on time with replenishments of our food and provision of frequent treats.

Occasionally they were late, but a few increasingly loud grumbling squawks usually led to them running to carry out their duties. Obviously, they still required some training. Visits from Mikey and Molly were especially pleasant. Running towards them or sitting on their knees always resulted in extra special seed treats. I think their training was complete. On particularly warm days under the light of the big yellow ball in the ceiling-sky Mikey would sometimes sit on the ground and I could climb up on his legs and settle down comfortably for a nap. Mikey and Molly squawked some strangely soothing, rhythmic sounds that felt like a gentle rocking in the air. It was quite relaxing. One of the big pesky hoomans would often come and join us and bring the mini hooman Maisy along. She could ruin the ambience when she crawled over and decided to pull on one of my feathers. Definitely some training needed there.

My rumbling tummy aches happened less often and thankfully after that mahoosive, painful poop, my hard poops occurred less frequently. Sometimes, I wouldn't have a moaning tummy before I was surprised by the sudden pop of a small hard poop that blew out of my vent. I sometimes found it more difficult to get up and go and run down to the food bowl in the morning. On those days it was usually better to sit in the warm, dark corner of the coop for a bit longer before waddling down the ramp to join the other girls.

CHAPTER 11

THE END

This morning I woke up and struggled to stand. Although, I tried and tried I couldn't push myself up off the floor of the nesting area of the coop. I decided to settle back for a bit of a longer doze before setting off to start my day. With my eyes fluttering open and then closed, I managed to push myself back further into the corner of the coop. I heard a noise as Hetty entered the nesting area and wandered over towards me. What The Cluck! There was nowhere for me to run. But, Hetty didn't bully me, she just pecked gently at my feet, gave a soft squawk and wandered off again. Result – I may have trained her to start being nice.

I flitted in and out of sleep and was vaguely aware of the other girls popping in and out of the nesting area. At one point, I'm sure Chucky pecked my comb but I didn't feel it.

My head fell forward, I didn't have the strength to lift it although I was pretty comfortable. I started to think about the things that had happened to me. I couldn't quite remember everything. I had met some relatively nice hoomans who had been trained to serve my needs. Mikey and Molly and Maisy were mini hoomans that I had trained fairly well. Running through the coop run area to reach the plentiful food and occasional treats had been fun and memorable. There was a crowded, noisy, dark, and then bright place somewhere in the back of my memories. Mostly though, I could feel the soft, green grass under my feet, the warmth of the yellow sun on my back, the scratching in paradise and the cosy, snuggly sleeps with my sisters in the comfortable coop. I had a name and I was loved.

I half opened one of my eyes and noticed a colourful, pastel shaded path leading out from the back of the coop where a wall should have been. I effortlessly stretched out my wings and felt strangely light as I stood and hopped onto the path. Feeling as if I was floating, I waddled over the spectral walkway, squawking along to a rhythmic bop bop bopping melody to where I'm sure I could hear Babs calling out to me…

THE EGG INDUSTRY IN THE UK

Did you know that all the hens that lay the eggs required for commercial sale including those for supermarkets and food production, are slaughtered at the age of 72 weeks, because their egg laying reliability drops. From regularly producing 6 or more eggs a week they may drop to between 4 and 6 per week. This means it is no longer profitable for the farmer to keep the hens. So, at 72 weeks old the hens will be sent for slaughter and the farms restocked with younger hens. Lying hen carcasses are sold cheaply due to the limited meat yield so they will typically be sold for dog food, baby food or the more budget processed foods produced for human consumption.

Traditionally the hens would have been housed in small battery cages, in often overcrowded and unnatural conditions. In 2012 battery cages were banned in the UK although so-called 'enriched cages' are still used. These have slightly more space but still do not allow the hens to exhibit natural behaviours. Due to more public awareness there have been improvements made to the welfare conditions for many hens and some may now be housed in barns or free range type enclosures.

Increased awareness of the plight of laying hens has contributed towards a growing number of rehoming organisations who will make arrangements with farmers to purchase and rehome the hens before they are due to go to slaughter. These organisations will rehome hens to people who can offer a loving home to the hens, enabling them to enjoy a retirement in back gardens, on allotments, on community farms or small holdings. Unfortunately, having been bred to relentlessly produce eggs some will not survive the trauma of rehoming or will pass away shortly after arriving in their new homes. Positively, many do go on to enjoy lengthy retirements in happy homes where they are loved and can enjoy their final fairly natural years before they travel over the rainbow bridge.

Please consider where your shop purchased eggs and food products containing eggs have been produced. If you have the space, consider rehoming a few rescue hens.

Sources for further information:

Fresh Start For Hens www.freshstartforhens.co.uk

British Hen Welfare Trust www.bhwt.org.uk

United Poultry Concerns www.upc-online.org

Chicken Rescue UK www.chickenrescue.co.uk

RSPCA Egg-laying hen welfare standards set by the RSPCA (rspcaassured.org.uk)

GOV.UK Poultry: on-farm welfare - GOV.UK (www.gov.uk)

Printed in Great Britain
by Amazon